Willowbank

In Search of a Name

by Alan Fennell

Sundown Squirrel and his friend Rainbow Rabbit had spent the morning enjoying themselves.

They were about to go home to Willowbank Glade in the heart of Moonshine Wood when they heard an unfamiliar voice.

"Coo-eee!" it called happily.

Sundown looked about him. Apart from the two youngsters there was no one else in sight.

"Coo-eee!" came the voice again.

The squirrel had very sharp ears, but try as he
might he could not see from where the sound came.
"Coo-eee! Up here!" The sound came from
above them, decided Sundown and as he searched
the branches a shocking thing happened.

Sundown was soaked to the skin and the sudden deluge made his teeth chatter.

"Look," shouted Rainbow, trying to stop himself laughing. "It's a dormouse. Up there!"

With a mightly leap, Sundown sped up the tree
and raced through the branches after the little
dormouse who was desperate to escape.
  Now if there was one thing Sundown was good at
it was running through the tree tops.

While Rainbow shouted encouragement from the ground, the dormouse twisted and weaved through the twigs, but Sundown stayed hard on his heels.

The dormouse then made a mistake. He sped along a branch from which there was no escape!

It was too far from the other trees and Sundown swooped out a paw to catch the playful dormouse's jacket.

"Drop him down to me," called Rainbow. "I'll hold him until you get down.

On the ground, Sundown looked sternly at the dormouse's cheeky face.

"What's the meaning of this?" the squirrel asked gruffly. "Who are you?"

"I don't understand," smiled the dormouse.

"Of course you understand," snapped Sundown angrily. "What's your name?"

The dormouse looked puzzled. "What's a name?" he asked.

"It's what people call you," put in Rainbow.

"People don't call me anything," replied the tiny creature.

Sundown suddenly felt sorry for the dormouse. He'd never heard of anyone not having a name.

Whenever the folks of Willowbank wanted to know something, they went to Grandfather Pen Badger for advice. The kindly old badger was in his usual place on the willow stump in the middle of the village.

"This -eh- somebody hasn't a name," Sundown said. "What can we do?"

"Give him one," replied Grandfather Pen at once.

"Right," decided Sundown. "I'll call him ... eh ... I don't know what to call him."

"How do we choose names? Why are we called what we are?"

"Well," the badger sighed. "In this part of the world, we are usually named as soon as we are born.

"You, Sundown," continued Grandfather Pen, "were born at the end of the day. Rainbow was born when the sun was shining through the rain, and the rainbow was the first thing his mother saw."

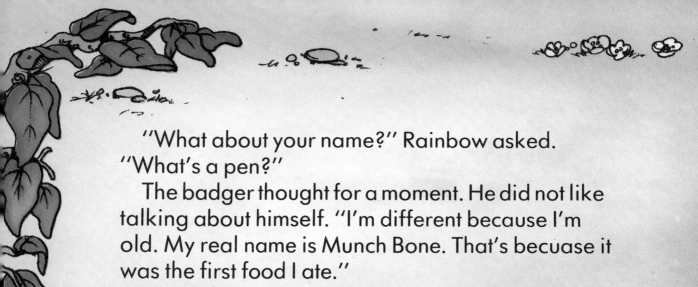

"What about your name?" Rainbow asked. "What's a pen?"

The badger thought for a moment. He did not like talking about himself. "I'm different because I'm old. My real name is Munch Bone. That's becuase it was the first food I ate."

Grandfather Pen looked sad. "My teeth are not sharp any longer," he went on, "so it would be silly calling me Munch Bone now."

" Then I started to write down the history of Willowbank, and soon everyone was calling me Grandfather Pen."

"We don't know what it was like when — thing — was born," said Sundown sadly. "How can we name him?"

"Watch him carefully," suggested the badger. "See what he does best and call him after it."

For the rest of that day, Sundown and Rainbow
followed the dormouse wherever he went.

"Perhaps he's a good tracker," wondered
Sundown as he saw the little creature sniffing the air.
"We can call him Hunter."

Then the dormouse started smelling the flowers.
"Huh! grumbled Rainbow. "That's not hunting."

"I caught him easily in the branches this morning," remembered Sundown. "That means we can't name him Swiftfoot."

"Maybe he has good eyesight," suggested Sundown, trying to find an answer to the problem. But then the dormouse ran straight into a tree.

"We certainly can't call him Hawkeye," giggled Rainbow.

While Sundown and Rainbow were thinking hard,
they suddenly lost sight of the dormouse.
"Which way did he go?" the rabbit asked.
"I don't know," replied Sundown. "Come on, we
can't give him a name if we can't see him."

Just then, a chuckling sound reached them.
"Coo-eee!" called the dormouse.
Sundown ran swiftly through the wood in the
direction of the voice. Next second he was flying
through the air . . . and SPLASH!

He had tripped over the outstretched foot of the
dormouse who had been hiding behind a tree.
"Grrr!" snarled the drenched squirrel. "Let me
get at him!"

With soggy clothes Sundown was very uncomfortable, but he chased after the dormouse. At last he caught him and held him high.

"The only thing you're any good at," grumbled Sundown, "is soaking me with water."

Then, slowly, a thought came to the squirrel. "That's it," he shouted in triumph. "We'll call you Downpour Dormouse."

Happily the three friends made their way back to Willowbank.

"I like my new name," said Downpour Dormouse.

"Good," agreed Sundown. "But I warn you. If you soak me once more people will be calling you something else . . . FLAT NOSE!"